To Charlie and Nita—
the exceptions to the in-law rule. Love you!

Elizabeth Bryan Mysteries

The Disappearing Card Trick

The Case of the Questionable Cousin

The Catnapping Caper

Ring Around a Mystery

Who Kidnapped Jesus?

The Secret in the Old Book

Cover illustration by Sally Schaedler

Copyright © 1998 Concordia Publishing House
3558 S. Jefferson Avenue, St. Louis, MO 63118-3968
Manufactured in the United States of America

Library of Congress Cataloging-in-Publication Data

Erwin, Vicki Berger, 1951
    The secret in the old book / Vickie Berger Erwin.
        p.   cm. -- Elizabeth Bryan mysteries : 6)
    Summary: Elizabeth explores an old house filled with books and encounters a mysterious boy trying to sell a first edition of a novel.
    ISBN 0-570-04995-4
    [Mystery and detective stories. 2. Christian life--Fiction.]
I. Title. II. Series: Erwin, Vicki Berger, 1951-   Elizabeth Bryan mysteries : 6.
PZ7.E744Sh   1998
[Fic]--dc21   97-28803
                                                                        CIP
                                                                         AC

1 2 3 4 5 6 7 8 9 10   07 06 05 04 03 02 01 00 99 98

CONTENTS

1
MOVING ON

"But why do we have to move?" Elizabeth asked.

Mom sighed and exchanged looks with Don Hamilton, her soon-to-be husband. "After the wedding, when Don moves in, we're going to need more room. We think we've found the perfect house, and we want you and Mike to come look at it with us." She looked at her watch. "The real estate agent is going to meet us there in 15 minutes."

Elizabeth stared at the pencil she was holding, turning it over and over. The thought of moving out of the only house she'd ever lived in made her stomach feel like it was turning over and over just like the pencil. She had so many questions that she didn't know where to begin.

"I like this house," Elizabeth's younger brother, Mike, said.

"We all like this house," Mom said, "but you'll like this new house too."

"A new house?" Elizabeth asked. "A *new* new house?"

Don shook his head as Mom answered. "New for us, but it's an old house."

Elizabeth had to admit she liked the sound of that. Her stomach started to settle back into place, then a terrible thought came to her. The pencil rolled off her fingers, across the table, and landed with a bounce on the floor. "Where," Elizabeth asked, "is this house?"

"That's the best part," Don said. "Neither one of you will have to change schools and your mom and I will still be close to work."

A small part of the weight Elizabeth had felt since Mom had announced that they'd found a house lifted. But she couldn't think of one house nearby that she'd want to live in that had a "For Sale" sign on it.

"Come see it with us. That's the first step," said Don, opening the front door.

It felt to Elizabeth like Mom and Don already had taken the first step. Mom hadn't asked her and

Mike to go look at houses. Nobody had asked them if they wanted to move. Elizabeth didn't remember Mom even mentioning that they were looking for a new place to live.

Mike folded his arms across his chest and stared at the floor. Don left his spot by the door and knelt beside Mike. "Just look at it with us, bud," he said.

"Everybody in the car," Mom said, the patience gone from her voice. She marched out the door and didn't look back.

Don scrambled up and followed. Elizabeth started toward the door more slowly, then stopped and went back to Mike. "We can at least go look," she said.

"Nobody will know where I live," Mike said. "And I won't know the way to school, and no one will be there to walk with me."

"We still live here," said Elizabeth. "Let's not worry about it before it happens." She took his hand and they walked to the car.

Don backed the car out of the driveway, drove to the corner, turned right, and pulled the car over before they'd gone two blocks. Elizabeth stared out the car window in amazement. She'd walked by this house hundreds, maybe even thousands, of times. It was one of her all-time favorite houses in the whole world. She knew that the woman who'd lived in it had died sometime during the winter. Because she hadn't seen a "For Sale" sign go up, she assumed someone from the family must be planning to move into it.

The house was Tudor style, white stucco with brown trim. A porch stretched across the front of the house and a garage peeked out from behind. The house was big—bigger than any house she'd ever thought about living in. She checked the house across the street and on either side, but this was the only one with a "For Sale" sign in the front yard. She wondered when the sign had been put out.

"What do you think?" Mom asked.

"It's big," said Elizabeth. It was the only thought she had that she could translate into words and that she was willing to share. She wasn't ready to tell Mom that she already loved this house—from the outside at least.

Mom and Don got out of the car, followed by

Elizabeth. Mike scooted across the seat and got out behind his sister.

"The house needs some work—some updating and a little paint," said Mom.

"But basically it's in good shape," said Don.

Elizabeth looked up, seeing the second floor, then the smaller windows on the third floor. "We can't afford this," she said.

Mom laughed. "We're selling two houses to buy this one," she said. Then she quickly added, "Or some one."

Don rapped on the door, then tried it. It swung open. "The agent must be here already," he said.

A curved staircase opened out of the entry hall. Three doorways led off the downstairs hallway. Elizabeth turned left and walked through a wide arch into the living room, still full of furniture. She wrinkled her nose. A damp, woodsy smell from the fireplace mixed with the scent of old grease and mildew. The fireplace was gray stone, large, with a dark wood mantel. Elizabeth ran her hand across the smooth, cool wood as she stared at the two overflowing bookcases on either side of the French doors leading into the next room. She passed through the doors and stood on the braided rug in the center of the smaller room. This was more than she'd hoped for. It was home.

There was a smaller fireplace in this room, a small sofa, and two leather chairs that were big enough to curl up in and fall asleep. The smell was familiar and comforting: ink, dust, leather, and a tinge of mildew. Taken all together, it meant books. She breathed deeply. Shelves lined the walls, and books covered every shelf—brown spines with gold, blue with black letters, red, black, and an occasional spot of yellow or white. It reminded her of Read It Again, the used bookstore where she worked after school. Overhead, Elizabeth heard the creak of wood as someone walked across the floor of the room above her.

"Great room, isn't it?" Mom said, joining Elizabeth. "And the rest of the house is just as great."

"How many bedrooms?" Elizabeth asked. Mike was already upstairs exploring, maybe even choosing his room. She started back the way she'd come. Through the window, she saw Don and Mike shooting baskets. Elizabeth looked up at the ceiling and asked, "Who's upstairs?"

"No one," said Mom. "We thought that Ms. Antoine was here because the door was unlocked, but she isn't."

"Ms. Antoine?"

"The real estate agent," Mom explained.

"But I heard someone walking upstairs just a second ago," said Elizabeth.

"Old houses, strange sounds. If we buy it, we'll have to get used to them," said Mom.

"Not creaks, footsteps," Elizabeth insisted. Mom shook her head.

Elizabeth backtracked through the living room, then hurried up the stairs. She hesitated on the top step, figuring out which room was above the library. When she located it, the door was closed. Elizabeth took hold of the doorknob and turned.

The door swung in quickly and hit against the wall. The crash caused Elizabeth to take a few steps backward. She approached the room slowly, put one hand on the doorjamb, leaned inside, and looked around. The room was small with a single metal-framed bed covered with a brightly colored patchwork quilt. A pillow with a white case rested at the head of the bed. There was a lamp burning on the bedside table and a small chest of drawers pushed against the opposite wall. The floor was shiny clean, and another braided rug was arranged neatly beside the bed.

Elizabeth stepped inside, but the room was empty. She opened the door on the far wall, expecting to find a closet, but it led into a bigger bedroom. There was no one in that room either.

"We may turn this bedroom into a bathroom," said Mom, coming up behind Elizabeth, "if we buy the house."

Elizabeth looked for a wall switch for the light, but there wasn't one. A book was on the bedside table, Jack London's *Call of the Wild*, and the pillow had an indentation, like someone had been leaning against it. "Who's here?" she called out.

"Elizabeth, I told you, no one is here," Mom said.

"Then why is that light on? And look at the pillow."

"Whoever showed the house last must have forgotten to turn the light off," said Mom. "And the pillow, I don't know what you're talking about."

Elizabeth stood very still and listened hard. She knew she'd heard someone in this room. She touched the pillow. It felt warm. Who had been here and where had that someone gone?

2

THE PINK
ROOM

"Lydia! Don!" a woman called from below.

"That must be Ms. Antoine," said Mom. "Look around up here awhile, and I'll be right back."

Elizabeth walked into the bigger bedroom. The double bed was high off the ground and had a tan headboard. It had a quilt covering it too. The quilt on the smaller bed was different squares of fabric sewed together, but this quilt had a pattern Elizabeth recognized from one of her mother's books—Wedding Ring. It was blue and white and beautifully stitched. The bigger bedroom was carpeted and had lots of old-looking furniture. She wondered if any of the furniture came with the house. It looked so perfect.

Out in the hall, Elizabeth opened more doors, each leading to a bedroom. One room in the back corner was papered in pink roses and had a canopy bed. There was a dressing table with a skirt that matched the pink bedspread, and a small bookcase was built into the wall. She knelt beside the bookcase and read some of the titles. Whoever had lived here before liked the same kind of books she did— Nancy Drew, *Little Women*, the Bible. Some of the other titles Elizabeth hadn't heard of, but the books looked interesting.

The room overlooked the backyard. Through the window Elizabeth saw a small pond and an overgrown garden. The pink bedroom was smaller than some of the other rooms, but she liked the cozy feel. It even had a small fireplace on one wall, though it looked like it wasn't used anymore. At least, no fires had been built in it recently. It was too clean. The closet was small, but there was a bathroom off the room. It had a huge bathtub that sat off the floor on feet that looked like a lion's paws. The linoleum covering the floor was curling up around the edges and there was no shower, but Elizabeth liked it anyway.

At the end of the hall there was another staircase with narrow, wooden stairs. Elizabeth started down. After a dozen or so steps, Elizabeth came to a landing with a door. She opened it and found herself in a small apartment. There was a sitting room with a sofa and a chair covered in flowered fabric, a small kitchen with miniature appliances, and a bedroom with windows that looked over the same spot of lawn as the windows in her bedroom. Elizabeth smiled, she couldn't believe she already was thinking of it as her room.

Continuing down the staircase, Elizabeth ended up in the kitchen. Mom must have had the kitchen in mind when she said the house needed some updates. The sink had two faucets—hot and cold. The cabinets were metal with spots of rust on them. Elizabeth opened one of the wooden doors leading off the kitchen, and damp, cold air came up from the basement. Another door led to a pantry and a swinging door opened into the dining room. Mom and the real estate agent, a small woman with dark hair and a nice smile, were talking in the front hallway.

"Elizabeth, this is Ms. Antoine. MaryAnne, our daughter, Elizabeth," said Mom.

"I've read about you in the newspaper," said Ms. Antoine.

Elizabeth felt her cheeks grow warm. She knew the woman must be referring to the accounts of the mysteries she'd solved.

"There's a basketball hoop outside and I made a basket," said Mike, running into the hall.

"He made a couple of baskets," said Don.

"Did you look at the house yet?" Mom asked.

"Don said I could have my own room here too," said Mike. "Upstairs."

"There's like five bedrooms up there," said Elizabeth.

"One for me, one for you, one for Mom, one for Don, and one for Aunt Nan," said Mike, counting on his fingers.

Elizabeth laughed at what her brother said, then the laugh died. Aunt Nan. How could they move away from the woman who had been like a grandmother to them ever since Elizabeth could remember. She didn't know how they would have gotten through her father's death if it hadn't been for Aunt Nan leading them to Jesus and His comfort. The light that had filled the house dimmed. "Will Aunt Nan move here too?" Elizabeth asked, her tongue so dry it stuck to the roof of her mouth.

"There's plenty of room for her, and we'd love to have her come along with us," said Mom.

"The apartment!" said Elizabeth. "Aunt Nan could have the apartment!"

"You've already found that, have you?" asked Ms. Antoine.

"We'd like Aunt Nan to have the apartment, but she isn't sure," said Mom.

"I won't come unless Aunt Nan comes too," said Mike. "I'd miss her cookies too much."

Elizabeth had the same feeling, but for different reasons. She'd miss everything about Aunt Nan too much.

"How did you get in the house?" Ms. Antoine asked.

"It was unlocked," said Don. "We thought you were here already."

"Someone must have shown the house and left it open. I'll have to check the log and see whom it was. We can't have that. There are some great antiques in here, and I'd hate for anything to happen to them." She shook her head.

"They left lights on upstairs too," said Elizabeth.

Ms. Antoine clicked her tongue. "So, what do you all think?"

Mom and Don looked at Elizabeth.

"It's pretty neat," said Elizabeth. "Do the books or any of the furniture stay?"

"We probably could work something out," said Ms. Antoine. "Mrs. Duncan's daughter, Kathy, died before Mrs. Duncan. The house was left to Kathy's son, Jim, but he's just a child. We're dealing with his stepfather." A crease appeared between Ms. Antoine's eyes.

"What about you, Mike? Do you like the house?" asked Don.

"Do we get to keep the basketball hoop?"

"I imagine that can be arranged," said Ms. Antoine with a laugh.

"I'd like to see my room," said Mike.

"Right this way," said Ms. Antoine, ushering Mike up the steps. She turned to Elizabeth. "You coming?"

"I think I'll have a look around outside." Elizabeth went back to the kitchen and tried to open the back door. It was locked, but there was a key sticking out. She turned it, and the door opened easily, leading her to the enclosed back porch. As soon as she was outside, she walked to the small pond and knelt beside it. There were gold fish swimming in the water. "Tiger and Dolores are going to love it here," she said to the fish, thinking of the fun her cats would have. They could each have a bedroom too, Elizabeth thought.

She looked up at the back of the house. There were more tiny windows under the eaves of the roof. The attic must be huge. For a moment she thought she saw someone or something move across one of the windows, but she made herself stop thinking about it. The only people in the house were her mom, her brother, Don, and Ms. Antoine. Old houses had lots of funny noises and shadows, and she'd have to get used to it. If they moved in— and she hoped with all her heart that they would.

"Hey, girl. You're trespassing," a gruff voice said.

Elizabeth jumped up and turned around. A man stood near the back steps, frowning at her.

"We're here to see the house," she explained, wondering why she had to explain anything to this man.

"Real estate agent here?" he asked shortly.

"Ms. Antoine?" Elizabeth asked.

"Any agent. I'm the owner of this house. They all have to deal with me," he said.

"She's inside with my mom," said Elizabeth. She wanted to go inside too, but she'd have to get past the man first.

The man, wearing a plain sweatshirt, jeans, and a baseball cap, took the steps to the back porch two at a time. Elizabeth noticed he also wore cowboy boots. He paused at the top of the short flight of steps and turned around. "You like the place?" he asked, pointing over his shoulder with his thumb.

Elizabeth shrugged. She didn't know much about buying a house, but she was sure she shouldn't tell the seller that she loved it and wanted it no matter what. She'd learned that working at the bookstore.

He opened the door and went inside. Elizabeth ran around and entered through the front door, reaching the hallway where her mom and Don were talking to Ms. Antoine at the same time the man did. Again, he frowned at her.

"Which one of you is the agent?" he asked.

"I'm Ms. Antoine," she said, stepping forward and holding out her hand. "And you are?"

"I'm the owner of this place. Pretty snazzy, huh?" He took off his baseball cap and turned around, craning his neck to see up the stairs.

"It's been a lovely property to show," Ms. Antoine agreed. Her hand, unshaken, dropped to her side.

"You people interested in making a deal?" he asked Don.

"We're discussing it," Don said, his voice tight.

"Mr. … I'm afraid I don't know your name," said Ms. Antoine.

"James," he answered. "Tony James." Mr. James walked to the archway leading to the living room and looked in. "I thought there were some books here, old books. Wait a minute, I see them." He stepped through the arch.

"There's more too," Elizabeth said. Mom frowned at her this time.

"*Is* he the owner?" Don asked Ms. Antoine in a low voice.

22

"The grandson is the owner, but this man may be the guardian. As I said, the boy's father and mother are both dead, and he's living with his stepfather. Someone mentioned that he's some kind of book dealer," said Ms. Antoine.

His mother and father were both dead. Elizabeth felt sorry for the boy that she didn't even know. To top it all off, he had to live with Mr. James, who hadn't made a very good first impression on anyone. He'd moved into the living room and was standing in front of the bookcase, pulling the books out one by one—like he owned them.

"Perhaps we should go back to the office," Ms. Antoine suggested. "I'd rather discuss your offer there."

Offer? Mom and Don were going to make an offer on the house? "We'll drop the two of you at home," Mom said to Elizabeth and Mike. "You won't be interested in any of this."

"Are we going to buy this house?" Mike asked loudly. Three adults quickly shushed him.

"Mr. James, we're leaving now. You'll lock up, I trust," said Ms. Antoine.

"Don't have a key," he said, stuffing a book back into place. "Think you could give me one?"

"Not without some identification," Ms. Antoine said.

"Good answer," said Mr. James. "I wouldn't want you handing out keys to my house to just anyone. I'll stop by your office and show you the papers I've got."

"We'll meet you there too," said Mom, "after we make a stop at home."

As Elizabeth climbed into the car, she looked back at the house one more time. It wouldn't be too bad to move here, she thought.

3

GREASY CREEK

"Teresa, you have to come look at some of the books at this house," said Elizabeth as she helped unpack a box of books. "There are lots of old ones."

Elizabeth blew dust off of a copy of Louisa May Alcott's *Little Men*. She loved her after-school job at Read It Again bookstore. Delivering books was fun, but the best part was straightening the shelves and unpacking the "new" arrivals. That's when she found the best stuff to read.

"Just because a book is of ancient vintage doesn't mean it's valuable," Teresa said. Her wiry orange hair was in its usual disarray, and her plaid jumper was streaked with dirt from the box of books she'd been unpacking. "Look. These specimens are an excellent example. Old, but nothing special." She sighed.

"I realize that," said Elizabeth. "But there might be something there, and what I saw was in great shape. Upstairs in the room that will be mine, if we get the house, there were some old Nancy Drew books with the dust jackets still on them."

"I can always make room in my humble establishment for something like that," said Teresa. "I have many customers who collect that series."

"The room I want has bookshelves built into the wall and a fireplace and ..."

The bell over the door rang, signaling a customer. Teresa stood up and smiled. "May I be of assistance?" she asked. Teresa never used one word when more would do.

Elizabeth reached up and smoothed her long, red hair, hoping it wasn't too tangled from her walk to the store from school. She straightened her vest and smiled at the young boy standing before the counter. He wasn't anybody she'd seen before, but she hoped she'd see him again. He looked about her age, maybe a little older. He was tall and thin and had straight, dark hair that needed a trim. He wore jeans, black Converse high-tops, and a gray sweatshirt with Indiana University written across the front in big red letters.

"Hi," he said. He set a book on the counter. "My grandmother sent me here with this book. She wondered if you'd be interested in buying it."

Teresa picked up the book and examined the front cover, then the back. She opened it to the title page, then flipped it over and read the print information. Elizabeth had seen her do these same things a million times. She stepped closer to see what the book was.

Teresa brought the book closer to her face as she read, then she fanned the pages of the book. "This is very nice," she said. "Your grandmother requested that you bring this in for an appraisal?"

The boy nodded.

"And why didn't she come herself?" Teresa asked gently.

"Grandmother is sick," the boy said. He gripped the edges of the counter. "I know this seems a little strange. She even said I might have trouble, but we need the money."

From time to time, people had brought stolen books into Read It Again to sell. Elizabeth knew that

27

was what worried Teresa about this book. Elizabeth didn't want to think that this boy had stolen something. He looked so nice. But she also knew that looks didn't determine whether someone was a thief. One of her own friends had been involved in shoplifting not too long ago.

"Did your grandmother mention a price?" Teresa asked.

"She said you'd know more about that than she does," the boy answered.

"What is your grandmother's name?"

"Betty," he said, clearing his throat. "Betty Kendall." Elizabeth didn't recognize the name.

"And you are?"

"Her grandson," the boy answered.

"Do you have a name?" Teresa asked, still speaking very gently.

"J—Jerry Kendall," he answered, stammering a bit.

"Do you go to school at North Middle School?" Elizabeth asked.

Jerry shook his head. "I go to private school," he said quickly. Elizabeth nodded. That explained why she didn't know him.

"This book is in very good condition," said Teresa. "And if it's what I suspect it is, it may be worth quite a bit of money. May I research it and get back to you?"

"I could stop by tomorrow afternoon," said Jerry, relaxing a little.

"Or I could call your grandmother," said Teresa, her eyes never leaving his face.

Jerry's face turned red. "We don't have a phone. Like I said, Grandmother has been sick for a while, and we need the money."

"Do you understand my position?" asked Teresa. "I don't know where or how you acquired this book."

"Look," said Jerry, reaching for the book, "it's signed to my grandmother. It says, *To Betty, Remembering the good times, Fran*. They grew up in the same town and this book is based on some of what happened as they grew up together."

"Your grandmother was acquainted with Fran Dolan?" Teresa asked.

He nodded. "It was a little town in Arkansas. This thing, this murder, happened when they were little, and the woman who wrote the book, her dad was a lawyer …"

"I'm familiar with the book," said Teresa. "I'm also fascinated that your grandmother was present as the events unfolded."

"It didn't happen exactly like in the book," Jerry said. "The author made up some of the stuff to make it a better story."

"Are you willing to let me do a little checking around?" Teresa asked. She laid the book on the counter. "You may take the book back with you."

Jerry's shoulders slumped. "How long will it take?"

"I can have an answer by tomorrow afternoon. If you can call back then …"

Jerry nodded. He picked up the book off the counter and tucked it under his arm. "I didn't steal it," he said in a low voice. "My grandmother gave it to me to sell. You must know that we need the money if she's willing to give it up. It was a hard decision for her."

"I'm sure it was," said Teresa. "I need to consult some reference materials to be able to come to a clear and equitable price arrangement."

"And you need to check with the police or someone," said Jerry, heading toward the door. "But you'll see, I'll be back tomorrow afternoon."

Elizabeth hoped he meant it. By then she'd be able to come up with something to talk to him about. So far she'd done nothing but stare at him and ask one stupid question. Of course he didn't go to North. If he did, she wouldn't have to ask. What private school did he go to? she wondered.

"You think he stole it, don't you?" Elizabeth asked as soon as the door closed behind Jerry.

"I must be suspicious to protect myself," said Teresa. "If I part with the funds necessary to acquire a book like that and then find out it belongs to someone else …"

"What book was it?" Elizabeth asked.

"*Greasy Creek*," said Teresa. "It won every major award the year it was published, and the author hasn't written a word since. If she has, it hasn't been published. If I'm correct, the copy this young Jerry has is a first edition and it's signed by the author, a valuable combination indeed." Teresa stared out the front window.

"I've heard of that book," said Elizabeth. "How

can you tell if it's stolen or not?"

"I'll telephone some of the other dealers in the area, consult the police and the phone directory." Teresa reached under the counter and pulled out a phone book. She flipped through it, stopping and running her finger down a column. "There's no listing for a Betty Kendall or anything close. But the number could have been unlisted before it was disconnected.

"Don't you have a meeting this evening, young lady?" Teresa asked.

Elizabeth looked at the clock. It was almost 5:30 and her Bible study group met at 6 P.M. She quickly gathered her backpack and purse. "Good thing you don't have any deliveries for me, isn't it?"

"When shall I see you again?" Teresa asked.

"I'll probably drop by tomorrow afternoon, after school," said Elizabeth.

"Ah, yes. Perhaps in time to re-encounter young Jerry." Teresa waved as Elizabeth rushed out of the store.

4

JERRY KENDALL AGAIN

When Elizabeth entered the fellowship hall at church, the first face she saw was Jerry Kendall's. He was standing at the refreshment table, eating a sandwich in big bites.

"Elizabeth!" Justin, one of her best friends from school, called to her from the other side of the room.

She waved at Justin, then looked at Jerry again, trying to decide whom she should speak to first. She felt someone standing behind her, then heard a whisper in her ear. "Who is that guy at the refreshment table?" her other best friend, Meghan, asked. Meghan was her best girlfriend, and Justin was her best boyfriend, in every sense of the word. Most of the kids at school considered Elizabeth and Justin to be "going out." Until Jerry, it had been a long time since she'd given another boy a second look. But there was something about this new kid …

"His name is Jerry Kendall, and he lives with his grandmother," said Elizabeth.

"How did you already find all this out?" asked Meghan.

"He came into Read It Again today to show Teresa a book." Justin was heading their way. Elizabeth waited for him. It would be easier to speak to Jerry with Justin along.

"Where have you been? I've spent what seems like the last hour trying to get away from Christy," said Justin. Christy was another friend of Elizabeth's. They'd known each other for years but had been part of two different groups until recently when Christy realized that people she'd thought were her friends were not good for her. Christy never missed an opportunity to get close to Justin. Sometimes it irritated Elizabeth, but not today.

"The guy over at the table," she said to Justin, looking at Jerry. "He's new and since you are too, kind of, you might want to go introduce yourself." At Christmas, Justin had told Elizabeth that he believed in Jesus as His Savior, as she did. He had started going to church with her family and even joined her church youth group. She still thanked God every night for sending His Holy Spirit to open Justin's heart.

"Who is he?" asked Justin.

"He came into the bookstore this afternoon. He lives with his grandmother," said Elizabeth.

"I wonder if he likes baseball," Justin said.

"Go ask him," Elizabeth replied. She and Meghan trailed along behind him to the refreshment table.

"Hi," Justin said.

Jerry turned quickly and upset the glass of lemonade sitting on the edge of the table. Everyone jumped back. Jerry's face turned a deep red. "Sorry," he mumbled. "I'll get something …"

Meghan already had a napkin and was on the floor, sopping up the sticky liquid. "It happens all the time," she said, smiling up at him.

"I'm such a klutz," he said, smiling back.

"I'm Justin Thayer." Justin stuck out his hand. "I'm kind of new here too. I thought you might like to sit with us for the meeting."

Jerry wiped his hand on his jeans, then shook hands with Justin. "Thanks, I'm …" His eyes met

Elizabeth's, and he dropped Justin's hand, then took a step back.

"Hi, good to see you again," Elizabeth said, trying to sound extra nice. She didn't want him to think that she thought he'd stolen the book. That was all Teresa.

"You too," Jerry said. "My grandmother thought it would be a good idea to meet some kids, and I called here to see if there was a youth group."

"We're glad to have you here," said Meghan. She'd finished cleaning the floor and slipped in between Jerry and Justin. Jerry towered over her. Meghan was petite, with long, dark hair. Her eyes were shining, and her cheeks were pinker than usual. Elizabeth thought she looked especially cute. From the look on Jerry's face, he thought so too. Elizabeth moved a little closer to Justin.

"This is Elizabeth and Meghan," Justin said.

"Jerry Kendall," Jerry said. "Elizabeth and I sort of met earlier."

"We'd better find a place to sit," said Justin. "There'll be time for us to talk again after the Bible study." Part of their youth group gathered every

Wednesday to read the Bible together and share a meal. Elizabeth loved it. Sharing the words of Jesus with friends really helped her live her faith.

They found four seats together, and Meghan offered to share her Bible with Jerry when he said he didn't have his along.

"Did you get the house?" Justin whispered.

"We're still waiting for Mr. James to decide," said Elizabeth. "He had 24 hours and he's using every minute of it. Mom and Don should know something by the time I get home."

Ms. Clark welcomed the group and opened the meeting with a prayer. Before Elizabeth knew it, the time had passed and they were getting ready to leave.

"You walking?" Justin asked.

"Mom doesn't want to leave the house, in case the real estate agent calls," said Elizabeth.

"I'm walking too," said Meghan.

"Hey, you guys." Christy walked up. "I had to sit on the other side of the room. Why didn't you save me a seat?"

"Sorry," said Elizabeth. "You already were sitting down."

"But I would have moved," said Christy. She turned to Jerry. "I don't think I know you. I'm Christy." She flipped her hair and flashed her dimples.

"Jerry," he answered.

"You need a ride?" Christy asked. "My mom is coming."

"I think we'll walk," said Elizabeth. She wanted to show Justin and Meghan the house they might buy.

"Mom said you were going to move," said Christy.

"We don't know for sure yet," said Elizabeth. "We've been looking at houses."

"I hope you move out in my neighborhood," said Christy.

Elizabeth smiled. "Maybe."

"I'd better go. Mom doesn't like to have to wait," said Christy. "Bye, Jerry, it's good to meet you. I hope I'll see you again soon." Jerry raised his hand and waved as Christy left.

"She didn't even speak to you," Elizabeth teased Justin.

"Another good reason to welcome Jerry," said Justin. Meghan smiled, but Elizabeth could tell it was hard for her.

"You walking home too?" Justin asked Jerry. "If you're going the same direction, you might as well go with us."

"Thanks," said Jerry. "I'm going away from downtown, west from Lindbergh."

"Great," said Justin, "that's the way we go too."

Jerry glanced over his shoulder toward the refreshment table. "Do you think they'd mind if I took a couple of those sandwiches home to my grandmother? I've been trying to feed her, but I know she's tired of soup out of a can."

"C'mon. I'll help you wrap up a couple," said Meghan. "And I know that my mother's group here at church would be glad to bring some food by for your grandmother. I'll ask her. That's part of what they do. If your grandmother goes to church here, I'm surprised they haven't already done it."

"They did," Jerry said quickly. "When Grand-ma first got sick. But she doesn't want to keep relying on people to bring food all the time. We've been doing okay. I came to stay for a while to help her out, until she gets her strength back."

Elizabeth decided she'd tell her mother about Mrs. Kendall anyway. Aunt Nan cooked constantly, and they always had more than they could eat. Jerry and his grandmother may as well enjoy some of it.

"Jerry, we hope you'll come back next week," said Ms. Clark as they left. "You might like to join our Sunday Bible class too. As you've already found out, we have a lot of nice people in this group."

Ms. Clark put her arm around Elizabeth and gave her a quick hug. "Plus, we have fun," she added. Justin moved quickly to avoid Ms. Clark's octopus arms, but Meghan hugged the group leader. When they were outside, Jerry paused at the end of the sidewalk.

"This is the way we're headed," said Justin, pointing.

"Okay, me too," said Jerry. "It takes me a few minutes sometimes to figure it out."

"You'll learn pretty fast. Are you already enrolled at North?" asked Meghan.

"North?" Jerry looked puzzled.

"The middle school," Meghan explained.

Jerry shook his head. "I'm going to private school."

Suddenly it struck Elizabeth as odd that Jerry could afford to go to private school but his grand-mother couldn't afford to pay for a telephone. She started to ask about it, but before she could, Justin asked whether Jerry liked baseball. He did and the two boys started speaking a language that she only partly understood. She understood a lot more now than she had before she became friends with Justin last summer.

Meghan and Elizabeth walked behind Justin and Jerry. "He's so cute," whispered Meghan. "And so nice." Elizabeth nodded.

"I wonder where he used to live," said Meghan. "Maybe we should invite him to go to the movies with us this weekend."

"We could do that," said Elizabeth.

"Do you think Justin might ask him?" Meghan asked.

"What about Rich?" asked Elizabeth.

"He can come too. And Christy always comes. I wish she wouldn't. You know she's going to try to get Jerry," said Meghan, looking glum.

"He smiled at you lots bigger than he smiled at Christy," Elizabeth said.

"You think so?" Meghan brightened a little.

Elizabeth nodded. "I'll talk to Justin about it."

"Hey, guys, I turn here," said Meghan, stopping at the corner of her street.

"Whoa, me too," said Jerry. "I almost missed it."

Elizabeth thought Meghan was going to burst, she looked so happy. "Thanks a lot for … you know …" said Jerry with a shrug and a one-sided smile.

"Anytime," said Elizabeth. "Hope we'll see you again, soon." Meghan and Jerry walked away—Meghan talking and Jerry listening.

Justin walked with Elizabeth to her house. "Hey, Mr. Hamilton's here. I need to talk to him about ball practice. The Astros need to start pretty soon to get in shape for the season." The Astros was the name of Mike's team. Don coached and Justin helped. That was how Elizabeth had met Justin.

"Come on in. Oh, no!" Elizabeth clapped her hand to her forehead. "I was going to show you the house we might buy. Maybe Mom will have an answer from Mr. James by now. You have to see it. It's huge and has a fish pond and a basketball hoop, a library, fireplaces. It's so cool.

"Mom!" Elizabeth called out as they entered. "Did you find out about the house yet?"

"Hi, Justin," Mom said, joining them in the hall-way. "Mr. James made a counter offer. And he thinks some of the books from the house are missing."

Mom's words turned Elizabeth's blood to ice. "What books?" she asked.

"I don't know a lot about old books," said Mom, "especially valuable old books. Some of the ones in the house are pretty pricey from what Mr. James says. He said some of the, what he called, 'modern first editions' are missing. He isn't sure that Mrs. Duncan still had them when she died, but he remembers seeing them at one time."

Elizabeth knew, from working at Read It Again, that modern first editions were books that had been published since 1940 (at least that's the date Teresa used). They were valuable for different reasons. *Greasy Creek* would fit in the category of modern first editions.

"So what do missing books have to do with whether you get the house?" Justin asked.

"Nothing at all, but Mr. James seems to think someone has been in the house going through things. Our real estate agent said that many people have looked at the house and that some people think any time a house is on the market they can open anything they want," said Mom.

"Which means that people have been going through things, but not necessarily to steal them," said Justin.

"That's what I think," said Mom.

"I can't figure out what house you're talking about. I've thought and thought and I can't picture it," said Justin.

"Then we'll have to take a little drive and show you. I wish we could go inside again," said Mom, "but we don't have a key. Don! You want to drive by the house and show Justin?"

"Mom, Justin doesn't want to drive by the

house," said Elizabeth, embarrassed that her mother was going to drag all of them out to the car and make Justin go see the house.

"I do too," said Justin. "I don't want you to move and not tell me where."

"Let me grab my coat and we'll go," Don called from the kitchen. "Go ahead and get in the car."

Justin opened the door and held it for Elizabeth and her mother. As embarrassing as it was, Elizabeth had to admit that she wanted to see the house again too.

Don and Mike joined them in the car. "Everybody buckled in?" Don asked.

"Prepared for takeoff," said Mike.

"When would you move?" Justin asked.

"We have to sell our houses first," said Don. "There's a teacher at the high school who's interested in buying mine and willing to let me stay in it until the wedding. Aunt Nan is thinking about buying the duplex."

"Mrs. Albright isn't going with you?" Justin asked.

"There's plenty of room," said Elizabeth. "She hasn't decided yet."

Don pulled up in front of the house. "There it is."

"It's huge!" said Justin.

"We can play basketball in the driveway," said Mike. "C'mon."

"Not tonight, bud," said Don.

Elizabeth stared at the darkened house. The biggest bedroom was in the front of the house, and she supposed Mom and Don would take it. As she was looking at it, the light came on. Although the blinds were drawn, a glimmer of light showed through. "Look," she said, pointing. As quickly as it appeared, the light went out.

"At what?" Mom asked.

"Nothing," said Elizabeth. "I thought I saw a light go on, but it was probably a passing car."

"It might be one of those timers that turns on lights when people aren't home. You know, the kind they use to make robbers think that someone is home," said Justin.

"Could be," said Elizabeth. Strange footsteps, missing books, lights in a deserted house—it all added up to another mystery.

5

THE CARE AND FEEDING OF JERRY KENDALL

The next afternoon after school, Elizabeth headed straight for Read It Again. She didn't want to miss Jerry—if he showed up.

"Hi, Teresa. Have you got anything for me today?" Elizabeth asked.

Teresa looked up from the yellow sheet of paper she was reading. "You can shelve some books for me, if you have time," she said.

"Anything interesting?" Elizabeth stepped behind the counter and stuffed her backpack and purse onto an already overflowing shelf underneath.

"Mr. Kendall has not returned, if that's what you mean," said Teresa.

"That wasn't exactly what I meant, but I did wonder," said Elizabeth.

"Peruse this." Teresa handed Elizabeth the yellow sheet. At the top it said, *Be Alert*. Under the bold letters, she read a warning for all used book dealers to be on the lookout for modern first editions that may have been stolen from the library of a recently deceased collector. A telephone number was listed at the bottom of the page for anyone to call with questions about books being offered for sale.

"My mother was telling me last night that the man we're trying to buy the house from thinks someone has stolen books out of it," said Elizabeth.

"Is he rather rotund and wearing cowboy boots?" Teresa asked.

"That's right. Mr. James."

"He's the individual who left the sheet here."

"Did you mention Jerry?" Elizabeth asked.

"I have no reason to believe that Jerry stole that volume," said Teresa. "His grandmother requested that he handle the disposal of it."

"Good," said Elizabeth. "What did you think of Mr. James?"

Teresa didn't answer.

"He accused me of trespassing and practically insisted that Don and Mom make an offer on the house right then," said Elizabeth. "He's a little pushy, if you ask me."

"He knows his books," said Teresa. "He purchased several very nice items from me, and I hesitate to gossip about a customer."

Elizabeth looked at her boss. Teresa might hesitate to express it, but she had an opinion. Elizabeth could tell by the way Teresa was busy doing nothing.

Every time the bell rang, Elizabeth looked up, expecting to see Jerry Kendall. Charles, Teresa's fiancé came by. A number of regular buyers, and a few new customers, stopped in to look around, but Jerry never showed up.

"Maybe when Jerry went home and told his grandmother that the book was valuable, she changed her mind," said Elizabeth as she gathered her things to go.

"Perhaps," said Teresa. "Or he may have found someone who didn't ask so many questions to buy the book first."

"I guess he could have," said Elizabeth. "I'll see you tomorrow."

The wind was brisk as Elizabeth walked home. She decided that she'd take a little detour and walk by her house. The first thing she saw when she stopped in front of the house was the "Sold" sticker plastered across the "For Sale" sign in the front yard. She turned and ran toward home. When she rounded the corner, Elizabeth hit what felt like a wall. Her backpack and purse flew out of her arms, and she landed on her bottom in the middle of the sidewalk.

"Are you all right?" Jerry asked, stooping to pick up her things.

It took Elizabeth a minute to catch her breath, then another minute to get over the embarrassment of the situation. "Fine," she said.

Jerry held out his hand, and Elizabeth grabbed hold. He pulled her to her feet, then handed her the backpack and purse. "I wasn't watching where I was going," he said. "I'm awfully sorry."

"I was running," said Elizabeth. "It wasn't your fault."

"Where are you going so quickly? You were moving like someone was chasing you," said Jerry.

"My house is a couple blocks away," said Elizabeth. "But we're looking at a house on this street. It has a sold sign on it today, and I want to see if it was sold to us or to somebody else."

Jerry glanced down the street. "I guess it's the big stucco house."

"Right. Do you live on this street?" Elizabeth asked, thinking it would be another reason to move into the neighborhood.

"I was just cutting through. I live a couple blocks over that way." Jerry raised, then quickly lowered, his hand.

"We thought you'd come by the bookstore today," said Elizabeth.

"When I told Grandma that the book might be valuable, she decided to keep it. I don't think she really wanted to sell it anyway," said Jerry. "Like I said, the author was a friend of hers."

"I was going to ask you when you came by Read It Again if you wanted to go to the movies with a bunch of us this Friday night. Justin, Meghan, Christy, and another friend, Rich, are all going. My mom will pick you up if you tell me where you live," said Elizabeth.

"That sounds like fun, but I'd better not. I don't want to leave my grandmother for long," said Jerry. "I'll see you at church on Sunday maybe." He started to walk off.

"Mom wanted to bring a casserole over for your grandmother, since she's sick," said Elizabeth. "Is that okay?"

"Maybe I could come home with you and get it," said Jerry. "Grandma doesn't like people showing up at the house. It's hard for her to get up and answer the door. Not to mention that I'm not a very good housekeeper." He smiled his lopsided grin. "But I know she'd like to eat something other than my cooking for a change."

Elizabeth didn't know how she could say that, he couldn't come home with her and pick up the food she'd already offered. Maybe Mom would insist that she drive him home. "Sure, that'd be fine," Elizabeth said, leading the way.

As usual, Don Hamilton's car was parked in the driveway.

"Your house is for sale?" asked Jerry.

"It wasn't when I left for school this morning," said Elizabeth.

Mom and Don met Elizabeth at the door. "We got the house!" said Mom. "Mr. James accepted our offer this afternoon."

"That's great!" said Elizabeth, hugging each of them in turn. "I walked by the house and when I saw the sold sticker, I was a little worried."

Elizabeth touched Jerry's arm lightly.

"Mom, this is Jerry Kendall," she said. "He's the guy I was telling you about from the Bible study. His grandmother is sick and you said you wanted to send some food over. Jerry came by to pick it up."

"Jerry, it's nice to meet you. Your grandmother is …?"

"Mrs. Kendall, Betty Kendall," he said.

"And she goes to our church?"

"I don't think she's an active member," said Jerry. He grinned. "But she makes me go."

"I know all about that," said Don, putting his arm around Mom. "But it's not a bad thing."

"Aunt Nan made a big pan of lasagna, and you can take some of that home with you. I have some salad and bread too," said Mom.

"Congratulations on your new house," said Jerry. "I'm sure you'll like living there."

"Hey, Elizabeth!" Mike barreled down the stairs, stopping at Jerry's feet. "Who are you?" he asked.

"This is Jerry. He's new in town," said Elizabeth.

"We're moving," said Mike. "I'm all packed." Elizabeth looked at the bulging backpack he had slung over his shoulder.

"We aren't ready to move yet," said Don. "Mr. James wants to close quickly, but we do have to sell a couple houses first. Jerry, it's nice to meet you. You don't play baseball, do you?"

"I do," said Jerry. "But I haven't since I moved here."

"We might be able to find a place for you. What position do you play?"

"I'm a shortstop, usually, but I can play anywhere on the infield," said Jerry.

"A good shortstop is something we can always use. Have you done any coaching?"

Jerry shook his head.

"I coach a couple of teams—Mike's and one for boys your age," said Don. "When the time comes, if you're still around, I'd like to give you a tryout."

"I'd like that. Justin and I were talking about it yesterday," said Jerry.

"I hate to run off like this, but I have a meeting at school. I'll be back later," said Don, giving Elizabeth's mom a quick kiss.

"Can you wait a second?" Elizabeth asked. "Mom has a bunch of food for Jerry and his grandmother. It'll be a lot to carry, so if you could drive him …"

"I'd be glad to," said Don.

"That's okay. You go ahead and go to your meeting. I don't mind the walk," Jerry said quickly.

"It's no trouble," said Don.

"Really. I can carry it," said Jerry.

"See you guys later, then." Don kissed Mom again and left.

"I'll get the food together," said Mom. "Elizabeth, could you help me? Mike, show Jerry your baseball cards, okay?"

Mike took Jerry's hand, and they climbed the stairs to Mike's bedroom. "I have a Stan Musial card that used to belong to my dad, but Mom doesn't let me keep it in my room. I do have an Ozzie Smith card," Elizabeth heard Mike say as they disappeared. Poor Jerry. She hoped he liked baseball cards.

"Elizabeth, there may be a reason that Jerry doesn't want anyone taking him home," Mom said as she transferred lasagna from a glass pan to a disposable aluminum pan.

Elizabeth couldn't figure out what her mother was trying to say. "What do you mean?" she asked.

"He may be embarrassed about where he lives."

It made sense. Jerry had guarded his address very carefully. When Elizabeth thought about it, she realized that he'd had on the same sweatshirt both times she'd seen him. "You may be right," she said. "I never thought about that because the first time we met, he said he went to a private school. Private schools cost a lot of money."

"He may be on scholarship," Mom said.

"Is there anything I can help you do?" Jerry asked from the doorway.

Elizabeth looked up quickly, her cheeks

warm, hoping that he hadn't heard them discussing him.

"Mike showed me all his cards and I thought I'd better get away while I could." Again, he grinned. When he did that, Elizabeth thought he was almost irresistible. Not so much as Justin, but close.

"What if we decide to stay here and watch videos one night this weekend?" Elizabeth asked. "Do you think you could come for a little while?"

"Maybe," said Jerry. "Grandma wants me to get out and make some friends. I don't want to be gone long though."

"Friday night? About seven?" said Elizabeth.

Mom handed Jerry a bag with pasta, bread, salad, and cookies in it.

"This is a feast," said Jerry. "Thanks so much. From me and my grandmother. I get kind of tired of my cooking too."

Mom patted him on the shoulder. "If you need anything, let me know."

Elizabeth walked Jerry to the door.

"I'll see you guys on Friday. This is one of the best places I've ever lived. Everybody's so nice," said Jerry. "Your dad is great."

"Dad? You mean Don? He's not my dad. My dad is dead. Don and my mom are getting married this summer, so I guess he'll be my stepdad. I wasn't too crazy about the idea at first, but he kind of grows on you," said Elizabeth.

"I have a stepdad too, but he's nothing like yours. I'd give anything ..." Jerry paused. "But there's no use wishing for things you can't change. That's what my mom always said anyway. May as well make the best of it. My stepdad is the reason I wanted to come here. I mean, I wanted to help Grandma too, but it gives us a little break from each other." He shrugged. "Enough of that. Thanks again for everything."

Elizabeth watched Jerry through the window. At the foot of the sidewalk he stopped and rummaged through the bag. He ate a cookie before he started off again. It gave her a little pang, right in the heart, to see him do that. She wanted to take care of him—and his grandmother—no matter where they lived. And she was determined to find a way to do just that.

6

ROW YOUR HOUSE ASHORE

"Teresa, you won't get any farther than right here," said Elizabeth, showing her boss the library at the new house. Mom had stopped by Read It Again to pick up Elizabeth for another look at the house and had invited Teresa to come with them.

Teresa's eyes were bright. "Only a cat could make it more perfect," she said as she walked around the edges of the room, running her hand over the spines of the books. Teresa owned a number of cats who had full run of the bookstore. In fact, two of her cats had been a big part of a mystery Elizabeth and Justin had solved.

"There will be three cats here before long," said Elizabeth, thinking of Tiger and Delores and Ozzie, Don's kitten. "I think I'll go upstairs for a quick look around again. Do you want to come or do you want to stay here?"

"I think I'll remain in paradise for a few minutes," said Teresa. "I may follow along shortly."

Elizabeth climbed the front stairs. She looked into the large front bedroom. It looked the same as it had a few days before. Opening the door to the smaller room off the big bedroom, she noticed that the light was off and the pillow was flat on the bed this time. She stepped inside to get a better look. The book that had been on the bedside table was gone. Elizabeth looked under the bed and on top of the dresser. She didn't see any sign of it. But Mr. James had been in the house, so he may have put it away.

When Elizabeth opened the door to "her" room and stepped inside, she heard a small splash. Looking down, she saw a narrow stream of water trickling across the floor. She followed it with her eyes to the bathroom. "Mom! Come here!" she yelled, stepping carefully around the water. In the bathroom, the water was running in a slow, but steady flow out of the wash basin. Elizabeth unplugged the sink and the water disappeared with a roar. She turned off the faucet.

"No!" she heard her mother say from the hallway. "I hope it didn't damage the ceiling."

"The sink drain was closed and someone left the water running," said Elizabeth. "I turned it off so there won't be any more water. It's like someone did this deliberately."

"I'll go down and see if there's a mop or some rags in the kitchen," said Mom. "We need to clean it up. I'll also check the ceiling in the apartment to see if it's damaged. This is something we don't need at all. I wonder if Mrs. Duncan's insurance is still in effect? I don't think we should have to pay for this. At least no one else will be coming through the house for a while."

Elizabeth stepped into the flooded bathroom, thinking she should check for rugs that might be soaking wet, but the bath rug was hung over the edge of the big tub. She stepped back into the bedroom to see if she needed to move anything out of the way, but all the rugs in the bedroom were pushed to one side. She looked around a little more and noticed that the books on the bottom shelf had been taken out and stacked on a top shelf. It was as if someone had made sure that nothing was in the way. Why would anyone do a thing like that?

Elizabeth heard footsteps on the front stairs, heavy footsteps, not at all like Mom's or Teresa's. She looked into the hallway. "Mr. James!"

"Sink leak?" he asked, looking at the water on the floor.

"Someone left the plug in the drain and the water on," Elizabeth said.

"Probably the same somebody who's been messing around with my books," said Mr. James.

"Your books?"

"Missing. Some of the best books in the collection are gone. I don't think Betty even knew they were valuable," said Mr. James. "There goes Jim's college fund."

"Mr. James! I didn't expect to see you here," said Mom. She was carrying a bucket and a mop.

"Good thing we showed up before the water caused some real damage," he replied. "I don't know about you, but I'm glad that a bunch of people won't be running in and out of here all the time."

"I agree. We'll have to have a little conversation about the water damage here. You'll want to check your insurance ..."

"It's not my house," said Mr. James.

"It's not ours yet, either," said Mom. "I'll take it up with Ms. Antoine."

"What do you mean? You thinking about backing out on our deal?" Mr. James' eyebrows came together, and his face turned dark red.

"We want the house, but we would like to have it in the condition it was when we signed the contract," said Mom calmly. She started mopping up the water in the bedroom, moving toward the bathroom.

"Insurance. I wonder if the books would be covered by insurance," Mr. James said.

"What a lovely collection in that library," said Teresa from the bedroom door. "What have we here, a celebration?"

"Not really," said Mr. James. "Someone flooded the bathroom. Aren't you the woman from the bookstore? Listen here, the books aren't part of the house deal. They're still mine, my son's actually."

"Teresa just came to see the house," said Elizabeth.

"Have any of you seen a young kid hanging around here?" Mr. James asked. "Tall, skinny, dark hair. I seem to have misplaced my son. He was supposed to be at home, but I called and he's not there." Mr. James laughed, without humor, as if he wanted them to think it was a funny situation. Elizabeth thought he looked mad rather than amused. She wouldn't want to be the son when he finally showed up.

"We haven't seen anyone," said Mom. "Maybe he's with a friend. Kids do that sometimes, especially if left alone."

"He's an independent sort. And he doesn't have that many friends," said Mr. James. "But you're probably right. He's probably hanging out with somebody and will show up when he's good and ready. I'll be heading back the first of the week, as soon as we finish up our business. I want to take some of these books out of here, though, before they disappear too."

"I'd be glad to discuss the future disposition of any of the volumes you decide to part with," Teresa offered.

"You want to buy them?" asked Mr. James.

"I'd like to discuss it," said Teresa.

"We'll talk, then," said Mr. James, nodding vigorously.

"I think we're finished here," said Mom, dumping water down the bathtub drain.

"I'll check the insurance papers about the water damage," Mr. James mumbled. "I want a nice family like yours to have this house. My wife loved growing up here. She always wished that we could move back."

"The ceiling in the apartment below has a damp spot and the flooring in here is coming loose," said Mom. "I'd like to have someone come look at it."

"Just make sure I'm here too," said Mr. James. "I'm staying at the Kirkwood Inn out by the interstate."

"Elizabeth, please take these back down and put them in the pantry in the kitchen," Mom said, holding out the mop and pail.

Elizabeth carried them downstairs. When she opened the pantry door, she noticed a smell, overpoweringly sweet, like food that had been left out to rot. When she stepped inside, she realized that the smell came from the waste can. Elizabeth pulled the bag out and tied it shut. Mr. James should know better than to leave trash for so long. There were fast-food wrappers, take-out cartons, and banana peels. She looked for another bag to use to line the trash can. On one of the shelves, Elizabeth found a loaf of bread, a jar of peanut butter, and a plastic knife. There were traces of peanut butter on the knife, as if someone had used it recently. There also were boxes of juice lined up. They were odd choices for a grown man to eat, but they had to belong to Mr. James.

Elizabeth took the trash bag to the front hall and set it beside the door. Then she went into the library to look at the book collection herself. When she entered the room, her eyes immediately landed on a familiar cover. *Greasy Creek*. It was a book she'd never seen before and now she'd seen it twice in a few days. Before she could pull it off the shelf, her mother called her.

"We need to leave if you're having kids over this evening," Mom said. "We still have to go to the grocery store and rent the videos. Teresa is waiting in the car."

"I'll be in touch," Mr. James said, showing them out the door. "What's this?" he asked, looking at the trash bag.

"It was in the pantry and kind of smelly," said Elizabeth. "I thought you'd want to get rid of it."

"Thanks," he said, looking puzzled. "I don't remember throwing anything away that would smell. Probably people looking at the house again.

"If you see my kid hanging around here, give me a call," said Mr. James. "You can be sure this will be his last trip for a while."

"Poor kid," said Mom as they got into the car, echoing Elizabeth's thoughts exactly.

7

SURPRISE!

"I can't believe it," said Mom, patting the car seat beside her after they'd let Teresa out at the bookstore. "I think I left my purse on the counter in the kitchen of the new house. We're going to be late, late, late."

"I'll run back and get it if you want to go ahead to the store," said Elizabeth. "Then I can go home and meet everybody when they arrive at the house. We don't have to start watching a video immediately."

"But what about …"

Elizabeth opened her purse and took out a $20 bill. "Money? I'll lend you this. I got paid this week." She opened the car door and stepped out.

Mom pulled a key marked with a red tag out of her pocket. "Be sure to lock up when you leave."

"What if Mr. James is still there?" Elizabeth

asked.

"Then remind him to lock up," said Mom. "I'll get soda, popcorn, frozen pizza, and two videos. Okay?"

"Get *Star Wars*," said Elizabeth. "We all like that one."

Elizabeth hurried down the street. There was no sign of Mr. James' car as she approached the house. All the lights were off and the door was shut. She stuck the key in the lock and turned. The door swung open and the hall light came on at the same moment.

Jerry Kendall stood at the top of the staircase, motionless, his eyes locked on Elizabeth.

"What ... What ..." Elizabeth stammered.

"Please don't tell anyone," Jerry said, his eyes as well as his voice pleading.

"Tell what?" Elizabeth asked.

"Come inside and close the door. Quick!" Jerry said.

"How did you get in here? What are you doing?" Elizabeth asked, closing the door, then leaning against it.

Jerry held up a key that looked like the one Mom had given her, minus the red tag. "This is my grandmother's house," he said. "I have every right to be here."

"Your grandmother? But you said …"

"That she was sick. She was sick, then she died. And she left me this house."

"Then Mr. James …"

"Is my stepdad."

Elizabeth didn't say a word.

"He's not a very nice man. He wasn't too bad while my mom was alive—strict, but not mean. Since she died, it's been different. I think he'd get rid of me if it wasn't for the money he thinks he's going to get from the house," said Jerry.

"Mr. James called his son Jim," said Elizabeth.

Jerry nodded. "I'm not his son. But my real name is Jim Duncan. He wanted to adopt me, but Mom never agreed. Jim James, wouldn't that be a great name?"

"You were here the first day when we came to look at the house, weren't you?"

"I hid in the attic," said Jerry/Jim.

"And the food in the pantry is yours?"

He nodded.

"And the water?"

"I thought maybe your mom would change her mind about the house if there was water damage. But I couldn't really do too much. I didn't want to ruin the books." He grinned. "I'm not very good at vandalism."

"Is the book in the library, the copy of *Greasy Creek*, the one you tried to sell Teresa?" Elizabeth asked.

Jim nodded. "I didn't think she'd buy it, but I was running out of money. If I could find what Grandma was talking about in her last letter, I'd be able to get away from here, from Tony, and he could have the house."

"What do you mean? Get away? How old are you? You can't be much older than I am," said Elizabeth, starting to worry. Now that she knew his secret, how much longer would Jim stay around?

"I'm 14," said Jim. "That's old enough. I can live on my own once I have a little money."

"Come home with me. We'll tell Mom …"

"No! You can't tell anyone," said Jim. He looked at the door, and Elizabeth knew he was thinking about running away again.

"Okay, I won't tell. I promise. What did you mean about your grandmother's last letter?" she asked. She'd figure out a way to make sure he stayed later. For now, the most important thing was for Jim to be safe.

"Gran was sick for a while. I kept hoping she'd get better and I could come live with her. I told her a few things about Tony, not the real bad stuff, though, like how he locked me in my room for three days so he could go to a book fair. He didn't want me to 'get in any trouble.' He left me with crackers, cheese spray, water, a box of cereal, and a couple of apples. I was only 8 or 9 years old at the time and too scared of him to think about getting away."

Elizabeth wanted to give him a big hug. How awful! She'd lost one parent. That was bad enough. But she still had her mom, and she'd never do anything as mean as Mr. James had done.

"Gran promised that I could come live here as soon as she got better. At the end, when she was so sick, Tony wouldn't even bring me here to see her. She'd written to me about a week before she died and told me not to worry about anything. She said she'd talked to someone and I wouldn't have to stay with Tony much longer. Gran said that she'd fixed it so Tony wouldn't care if I stayed with him or not. She ended the letter by saying she'd write more details later, but her nurse was insisting she needed to rest awhile. It was the last letter I got.

"Gran knew and I knew that the only reason Tony was keeping me was because he thought I was going to inherit a lot of money. And the books. One thing about the guy—he does know about books. I've listened and learned. All I need are a couple good books from Gran's library and I'll have it made. If I can convince anybody to buy them from me, that is. Your boss isn't the only one who's suspicious of how I got a hold of the books I've tried to sell. Then Tony took that notice around." Jim looked over his shoulder.

For a moment, Elizabeth thought he was going to turn and run. She started toward him, but he sat down and covered his face with his hands.

"Do you have any idea what your grandmother meant by what she wrote in the letter?" Elizabeth asked softly.

"No. I need to find out who her lawyer is,

who's handling her will," said Jim, dropping his hands.

In the harsh light of the hallway, Elizabeth noticed that he had dark circles under his eyes. He rested his elbow on his knee, then leaned his chin on the palm of his hand.

"Maybe I can find out," said Elizabeth. "Mom and Don are buying the house, so the lawyer may be involved. Plus, with the water damage, they want to check the insurance. Are you sure you've looked everyplace that your grandmother may have kept papers? Maybe she wrote the letter and didn't mail it."

"I've looked in her room, in her desk, in all the drawers around the house. I have to be on guard every minute because I never know when someone is going to come in," said Jim. "I was actually asleep the afternoon your family came in to see the house. It's a wonder you didn't walk in and find me conked out."

Elizabeth smiled at him. "I knew I heard someone walking upstairs, but my mom insisted it was old house noises."

"That's me, an old house noise." Jim's return smile wasn't very big.

"Come home with me and watch videos like we've planned. You can have something to eat, as much as you want, and I'll try to figure out a way to find out about the lawyer. Maybe there's a new will. I don't know how it would be set up, but I'll bet your grandmother could have fixed it so Mr. James couldn't touch your money," said Elizabeth.

"So you're a lawyer now?"

"No, but what else could she mean?" asked Elizabeth. "Will you come? I promise, on my honor, not to tell anybody you're staying here. And now that I know, I can make it easier for you. I'll even lend you some money, if you want. After all, you're going to be rich." She smiled to let him know she was teasing.

"Not if Tony gets his hands on the money first. I think he's been kind of looking for something too. He knew Gran wasn't happy with him. Gran wasn't the kind of woman who kept her mouth shut." This time Jim's smile spread from one side of his face to the other and lit up his eyes too. "She wasn't a bit quiet."

"Will you come?"

Jim stood up. "Don't forget to call me Jerry. If Tony's told anyone my name, I don't want them to even suspect I'm the runaway bad guy."

"I won't forget. And what do you mean, *bad guy*?"

"I'm sure that's the way Tony's painted me," Jim answered.

"I have to grab my mom's purse. It's on the counter in the kitchen," said Elizabeth. By the time she returned, Jim was waiting at the front door.

"You want to leave a light on?" Elizabeth asked, then clapped her hand over her mouth. "I guess not."

"I guess not," Jim echoed.

8

SEARCH PARTY

When Elizabeth woke up on Saturday morning, her first thought was of Jim. She said a quick prayer, asking Jesus to watch over him. She couldn't imagine being on her own with no one to turn to. She thought about all the adults who cared for her—Mom, Aunt Nan, Teresa, Don, and Pastor Jim, the man who'd helped her so much when Dad died. Then there were her friends—Meghan, Justin, Rich, Amy Catherine, even Christy. She was truly blessed. "Thank You, God," she whispered.

Since she was the only one Jim had confided in, Elizabeth knew she had to help him. While they watched movies the night before, Justin had asked her why she was so quiet. She didn't know how to answer because she'd been thinking about Jim. Jim had been busy the entire evening—eating.

Elizabeth got out of bed. She'd agreed to meet

Jim at his grandmother's house. She dressed in jeans and a sweatshirt, then pulled her hair back into a ponytail.

There was a note from Mom on the table when Elizabeth came downstairs. "Took Mike to baseball practice. If you want to go out to lunch with us, come to the park when you get up. You'll be able to find us. Love, Mom." Elizabeth felt relieved that she didn't have to explain anything to her mom. Maybe Jim would come with her when they finished looking around the house some more. He could eat another good meal. Just in case he wouldn't, Elizabeth made a couple ham sandwiches, chose some apples and cookies, then stuck everything in a bag.

Elizabeth didn't bother with a jacket. It looked and felt like spring outside. The trees were beginning to bud and some of the flowers were blooming. She was tired of winter and putting on all the clothes necessary for the shortest trip anyplace. She enjoyed the weather on the short walk to her new house, managing to make the trip without encountering anyone she knew. When Elizabeth arrived at the house, she went around to the back door.

There was a doorbell that was pulled away from the doorjamb and rusted around the edges. It looked like it shouldn't work, but Jim had assured her it did. Elizabeth pushed it and held it in for one long buzz, then she let go and gave it two more short punches. The back door opened, seemingly on its own. Elizabeth stepped inside, the door closed, and Jim was there.

"I feel like I'm in the middle of a Nancy Drew mystery," said Elizabeth, looking over her shoulder. All the secrecy was making her hypersensitive to the slightest noise. She just knew she'd heard someone behind her, but when she looked no one was there. She decided it must have been the rustle of leaves in the slight breeze.

"I know what you mean. Wait until we start going through stuff here in the house," said Jim. "It's even more like that."

"Do you still have your grandmother's last letter?" Elizabeth asked.

"Tony has it," said Jim. "I think he wanted to make sure that nothing even hinted that the estate would go anywhere but under his control."

"Was your grandmother in the hospital when

she died?" asked Elizabeth.

"She was sick, but no one expected her to die when she did. She was here at home, alone." Jim swallowed hard. He was staring at the floor.

Again, Elizabeth wanted to give him a big hug. She had a feeling he was wishing he'd been with his grandmother. Or that someone had been there. She hoped he at least had the comfort of knowing his grandmother was in heaven.

"What did she like to do?" Elizabeth asked.

"Gran read a lot," said Jim. "She loved books, as you already know. She liked popular fiction, history, children's books, just about everything except science."

"Did you look through any books to see if she'd stuck something inside one of them?" asked Elizabeth. She set the lunch sack on the counter.

"What's that?" Jim asked.

"Some food, just in case we get hungry," said Elizabeth.

Jim opened the sack. "Is it okay if …?"

"Go ahead. I had something before I left home, but I didn't know how long we'd be here.

Mom said we could meet them at the park at lunchtime and go out to eat. Mike has ball practice so Don and Justin will be there too."

"You told your mom you were coming here?" Jim's words were almost unintelligible, his mouth was so full of ham sandwich.

"They already were gone when I got up. She left a note. I thought we might at least take a break around lunchtime and go meet them. If you want to," said Elizabeth.

"I don't know." Jim finished the sandwich and reached inside the bag again. His hand came out empty. "I'll stick this in the fridge for later. I feel like I've been eating at your house a lot."

"My mom loves to feed people. Aunt Nan likes it even more," said Elizabeth.

"We'll see. Want to start the search?" Jim closed the refrigerator door and headed toward the back stairs. "Gran didn't come downstairs much toward the end, so I figure anything she may have been working on was upstairs."

"But someone may have moved any books she was reading down here," said Elizabeth, pausing in the hall.

"You want to look around in the library a little?" asked Jim. "I thought I'd go through her desk again. This sounds kind of way out, but maybe there's a secret drawer or something that I didn't find the first time I looked at her papers."

"I'll check with you in a while," said Elizabeth. She turned off the hallway and went into the library. There were so many books she didn't know where to start. Jim had said his grandmother liked fiction, children's books … Elizabeth wondered if she should check the books in "her" room. Those were all children's books, and Mrs. Duncan may have had them with her or gone in there to read them. Elizabeth knew she had to decide on a place to start and do it. She didn't want to get off track running here and there. She decided to start beside the fireplace and go around the room.

Elizabeth pulled down one book after another, fanned the pages, and put it back. Mostly she found dust. Her mouth felt dry and her eyes itched from all the particles flying around in the air. She finished one bookcase and moved to the next.

When she'd gotten about halfway down that

case, a paper floated out of one of the books and landed on the floor. Elizabeth picked it up and unfolded it. It was a letter from Fran Dolan, the author of *Greasy Creek*, the book Jim had brought into Read It Again to try to sell. Elizabeth scanned the text. It had been written quite some time ago, when Ms. Dolan was still working on the book. Elizabeth didn't know for sure, but she had a feeling that the letter by itself might be worth something. It talked about the event the book was based on and asked Mrs. Duncan if she remembered how a certain thing had happened. Elizabeth laid it on the shelf to show to Jim. If he'd let her, she'd take it in to Teresa.

Elizabeth heard a pounding on the stairs. She stepped into the living room and met Jim in front of the fireplace.

"Quick!" he said, grabbing her by the wrist. "Tony's coming!" Jim pulled her up the stairs. He opened a narrow door and practically threw Elizabeth inside. Jim followed, shutting the door and locking it behind them. He pulled a penlight out of his pocket and shined it on the narrow wooden stairs. "The attic," Jim whispered. "Go on up."

Elizabeth tiptoed up the stairs, each creak sounding deafening. There were windows that let in the spring sunlight once they made it to the top. The room was full of … all Elizabeth could think of was *stuff*. There were boxes, trunks, picture frames, furniture, mattresses, and lots and lots of dust.

"Have you looked around up here at all?" Elizabeth whispered.

Jim shook his head and put his finger over his lips.

Elizabeth walked as silently as possible over to the window and sat down, watching for Mr. James to leave. Jim stationed himself on the opposite side of the room, looking out a back window.

After what seemed like a long time, Elizabeth joined Jim. "Did you find anything?" she whispered. He frowned at her as he shook his head.

"I found a letter," she said. Jim's head jerked up and looked at her, his eyes wide.

"Not about you," Elizabeth said, "but I think it's valuable. It's from Fran Dolan, talking about *Greasy Creek*. The letter was stuck inside a book."

"What did you do with it?" Jim whispered.

A huge, big knot lodged in Elizabeth's stomach. She'd left the letter on a shelf in the library. The library was always the first place Tony James went.

"What?" Jim asked, a little louder.

"I left it in the library," Elizabeth mumbled.

"Don't worry about it. I don't really care about the letter. I want something from my grandmother that says I don't have to live with Tony anymore. Although, I don't know where else I could live," whispered Jim. He turned back to the window.

Elizabeth returned to her window, wishing Jim had another place to go too.

THE SECRET OF NANCY DREW

It seemed like hours before Mr. James finally walked out of the house. "He's leaving," said Elizabeth, standing and stretching.

"Don't go down yet," Jim cautioned. "Sometimes he comes right back or he only goes out to his car for something."

"He has some books with him," said Elizabeth. "Can he just take them out of the house like that?"

"Who's going to stop him?" asked Jim.

Mr. James climbed into the car and pulled away from the curb.

"Can we go downstairs now?" Elizabeth asked.

Jim didn't bother to answer. He clumped down the steps and unlocked the door, holding it for Elizabeth to go through first. "I leave the key on the inside," he said, "so Tony can't get in here. A couple times I've heard him try the door.

"My biggest fear is that he'll come in some night when I'm sleeping. There are times that I've fallen asleep and been awakened by a noise. Those times, I freeze up and can't move, thinking it's him. That's what happened the afternoon you came to look at the house," said Jim.

"It would have been like Goldilocks and the Three Bears if we'd found you sleeping in the bed," said Elizabeth.

"It would have been more like Robin and the Three Hoods," said Jim, grinning. "And I'd be more like one of the three hoods. But I'm not much like Goldilocks either."

Elizabeth giggled.

"It's nice to have somebody to talk to for a change," said Jim. "You going back to the library to look some more?"

"Come with me, and we'll see if Mr. James took that letter," said Elizabeth.

Elizabeth went directly to the shelf where she'd left the letter and, as she had expected, it was gone. "I'm sorry," she said. "I should have brought it with me or put it back in a book."

"Tony can have all the books and letters and money he wants if I don't have to go back and live with him."

"Isn't there anybody else? Another relative? A friend?"

"Tony tries to make sure I don't make many friends. I had a math teacher I liked a lot in junior high school, but he got a better job someplace else. He knew how much I hated living with Tony, but Gran was still alive, and I still hoped that I might be able to come live with her someday," said Jim. "Whenever I made a friend at school, Tony called his parents and warned them not to let their son hang around me too much or some of the badness might rub off. I never did anything that anyone would consider bad. What he'd do is make up things and scare the parents to death. What parents wouldn't be worried if another kid's dad called up to tell them how bad his kid was?"

"He did that?" Elizabeth had a hard time believing that someone could be so mean.

"When I didn't have any friends, he had me all to himself. I had to take care of the house, which I didn't mind much, and help him load and unload boxes of books. I even learned a little bit about the book business. I probably would have liked it if I hadn't been doing it with Tony. When Mom was alive and we went to book fairs, it was fun," said Jim. "Anyway, we'd better get back to work."

"Why don't you stay down here and help me go through the rest of the books? There may be other letters from Fran Dolan. If there are, I'll take them to Teresa to see if they're worth anything. In fact, I bet I could talk her into buying *Greasy Creek* now," said Elizabeth. "I could tell her I met your grandmother."

"I don't want you to have to lie too," said Jim. "I know it's wrong. My mom used to take me to church. Right now I'm wondering where Jesus is hiding. I don't think He's watching over me very carefully."

"He is!" said Elizabeth. "You can believe that. And you can ask Jesus for His help. I've been talking to Him about you."

"You mean I should pray?" asked Jim. "I don't think that's going to help me now."

"You'll never know unless you try." said Elizabeth. "Since Jesus loved you enough to die for you, don't you think He loves you enough to want you to have a good home?"

Jim turned away and started going through books, one by one. Elizabeth decided she'd said enough for now. She whispered a prayer of her own and finished the section of the bookcase she'd started before they went to the attic to hide from Mr. James. "Do you mind if I go upstairs and look in some of the children's books up there?" she asked.

"Go ahead. There's a whole bunch in my mom's old room," said Jim.

"The pink room? Looking out over the fish pond?"

"That's the one."

"If we move in here, that's the room I want. Your mom and I like the same books," said Elizabeth.

"*Little Women*? Nancy Drew?" asked Jim. "She was a Nancy Drew fanatic."

"*Little Women* is my very favorite and my mom's too."

"It was my mom's and Gran's favorite," said Jim. "They always wanted me to read it, but I never quite got caught up in the story."

"I guess I can understand that. I never liked *Call of the Wild* that much," said Elizabeth.

"That's what I just finished reading," said Jim.

"I saw it when we were looking at the house that first day. It was on the table beside the bed."

"It was good. You should read it."

"I'll read it," said Elizabeth, "when you read *Little Women*."

"We can talk about it," said Jim.

The first thing, Elizabeth did when she got upstairs was pull *Little Women* from the shelf. She'd give it to Jim before they left. And they should leave soon, she thought, looking at her watch. It was getting close to lunchtime. Mr. James had kept them from doing a lot of things they'd planned on doing. There was no way they'd get through all the books that day, and somehow, Elizabeth thought, that was where they might find something.

Mrs. Duncan's copy of *Little Women* was old. Elizabeth could tell from the picture on the front cover. She opened it for a look at the illustrations. The book was even older than she'd first thought. Inside, the illustrations were what Teresa called "tipped in," meaning that the pictures were glued onto the pages. There were little pieces of tissue paper between the printed page and the illustration. This was another valuable book that Jim should show to Teresa.

Elizabeth moved on to the old Nancy Drew books. As she'd mentioned to Teresa, they still had dust jackets that were in great condition. As Elizabeth thumbed through a book, she thought it might be fun to compare one of the old editions with the editions she had on her bookshelf. Maybe Jim would let her borrow one of the copies overnight.

She lined up the different copies and chose *The Secret in the Old Clock*. It was the very first volume in the series. Elizabeth started reading. She turned a page and found another sheet of paper. She unfolded it. *Dear Jim* were the first words on the page!

10

AN ANSWER TO PRAYER

Elizabeth read through the letter quickly, her heart beating faster with each word. "Jim!" she shouted when she finished. He didn't answer, but she heard his footsteps on the stairs.

"The neighbors are going to hear you," he said, joining her beside the bookcase.

"I found it. I found the letter you need. It's all right here, the lawyer's name, what your grandmother planned to do, everything," said Elizabeth, holding the letter by a corner. "She must have been reading this book before she died."

For a moment, Jim didn't do anything but stare at the paper hanging in the air. Suddenly he grabbed for it, making Elizabeth jerk away and drop the letter.

"Sorry," she said, leaning down to pick up the letter at the same moment Jim did. Their heads bumped and Elizabeth ended up sitting on the floor, rubbing her forehead.

"That was like a brick wall running into a brick wall," said Elizabeth, laughing. The bump hurt enough to bring tears to her eyes, but she was laughing at the same time.

"The letter's under the bookcase now," said Jim. He laid down on his stomach and reached under the low shelf with his fingertips. Slowly he worked the paper out.

"Read it," said Elizabeth, scooting across the floor and leaning against the footboard of the bed.

"She appointed another guardian for me, her lawyer," said Jim. "And she set up a trust account so Tony couldn't get at the money. All I have to do now is talk to this lawyer. Do you know her?"

Elizabeth shook her head. "My dad was a lawyer, but he's been dead for quite a while so I don't know many lawyers. I could ask Mom and Don."

"No! Don't say anything to them yet," said Jim. "I want to make sure this lawyer thing works out. I don't want to have to go back to Tony."

"If it doesn't work out, what are you going to do?" Elizabeth asked.

"I'll find a way to take care of myself," said Jim. "Don't worry."

"But …"

"It's different for me than it would be for you," said Jim. "I'm used to relying on myself. Besides, this is going to work out. I know it is." He folded the letter and put it in his pocket. "I'll call the lawyer, she'll help me."

It's Saturday, Elizabeth thought.

"Can I use your telephone?" Jim asked. "Or I could go use a pay phone." He stuck his hand in his pocket.

"You can use mine," said Elizabeth, getting up. "Now?"

"You're going to miss lunch with your mom and dad, I mean, Mr. Hamilton. And Justin." Jim smiled when he mentioned Justin.

Elizabeth felt her face get hot. "We're friends," she said quickly. "Come to lunch with us, then you can go home with me and use the phone."

"Go on to lunch. I think I'll go use the phone by the train station. I may drop by the lawyer's office." Jim started out of the room.

"I know that Mom and Don …"

"I want to do this now, Elizabeth. I've been waiting and waiting for something, some sign that somebody cared about me. Now that I've found it, I can't put it off any longer," said Jim.

"It's the prayers," said Elizabeth.

"What?"

"It's an answer to our prayers," she said. "I told you if you asked Jesus, He would help you. Did you pray?"

"I did, but it wouldn't have happened that fast," said Jim.

"Don't argue with God," said Elizabeth, trying to look stern.

"I guess I shouldn't," Jim said.

"Will you let me know what happens?" Elizabeth asked.

"Sure, as soon as I know something." Jim walked with her to the back door. He looked through the window before opening the door.

"I'll talk to you later then," said Elizabeth. The door closed behind her, and Jim disappeared into the shadows of the house before she'd finished speaking the last word.

11
THINGS THAT GO BUMP IN THE ATTIC

Elizabeth waited by the phone all afternoon. It didn't ring once. She had her math book open in front of her, but she didn't turn even one page. As it began to get dark, Elizabeth started to worry. What if Jim hadn't found the lawyer? What if Tony had showed up, trapping him in the attic for the entire afternoon? She pulled out the telephone book and looked up the name she remembered from the letter.

Elizabeth punched the buttons on the phone, then listened to it ring. Surely lawyers had emergency numbers. What if one of their clients were arrested? "Hello, you've reached the law office of Baker and Ingram. We're closed for the day. Our regular office hours are 9 to 5, Monday through Friday, and 9 to 12 on Saturday. Have a nice weekend!" There wasn't even a beep at the end of the recording so a caller could leave a message.

When Elizabeth stood up, the phone book slid off her lap with a thump. She couldn't stay in the house one more minute wondering what Jim was doing. She grabbed a jacket, knowing that it would be cooler outside as evening approached, and called out to her mother, "I'm going for a walk! I need some fresh air."

"Be back in time for dinner," Mom answered.

Elizabeth didn't walk, she ran the short distance between her house and the Duncan house. There were lights burning in the master bedroom upstairs and in the library. She slowed, expecting to see Tony's car parked on the street. When she didn't, she rounded the side of the house and buzzed the doorbell in the code she and Jim had prearranged. The door remained tightly shut.

The screen door opened easily and Elizabeth walked across the back porch to the inside door. It was ajar. She knocked, but no one answered. "Anybody here?" she called out. "It's me, Elizabeth."

The open door, partnered with no answer from inside the house, set off alarm bells in Elizabeth's head. She stepped inside. A crumpled paper bag was on the floor beside the kitchen sink. An apple core teetered on the edge of the counter. The light from the library beckoned.

Elizabeth crept down the hallway and stopped at the entrance to the library. She covered her mouth with her hands. Every book had been taken off the shelves and thrown on the floor. She picked up a few that had opened as they fell, creasing pages. Everything told her she should leave right then and there and get help. But she didn't.

The living room looked undisturbed so she headed up the stairs. Every book in the house was on the floor. Bedding was ripped off of beds, and papers were strewn all over the bedrooms.

As Elizabeth knelt on the floor in the pink bedroom to pick up the copy of *Little Women* she liked so much, she heard a thump. For a moment she wished she could make herself small enough that she'd disappear, then she looked around frantically for a place to hide. The thump sounded again, louder this time. Then she heard a series of knocks and bumps that sounded like something rolling down the attic stairs.

"Jim!" Elizabeth called out. A series of knocks answered her call. She ran to the attic door and pressed her ear against it. Another thump caused the door to vibrate and Elizabeth to step back. "Just a minute. I hear you," she said. She tried the door, but it was locked. "You have to unlock it!"

There was another series of thumps. Why wasn't he talking? Was it even Jim? She heard a humming, two hums.

"You're scaring me!" she said against the door. "And it's locked. I can't get it open. What should I do? Talk to me, Jim, talk to me."

Again she heard the awful humming sound, followed by thumps on the other side of the door. "I'm going to get my mom."

At that, Elizabeth thought he was going to kick the door down. The key. Where was the key? If it was on the other side of the door, maybe Jim could somehow unlock it. "Is the key in there? Knock against the door once if it is and twice if it isn't," she said. Two quick bumps followed.

Keys. Where did people leave keys? Elizabeth ran to the kitchen. Her mom had a drawer full of keys. No one remembered what they unlocked, but Mom was worried they'd need one of them someday so she kept them.

She pulled out the drawers one at a time, not worrying about what fell out as she slammed each one shut after quickly examining the contents. Elizabeth hit the jackpot on the third drawer down. There was a jumble of keys and some of them looked as old as the one she'd seen in the attic door earlier in the day.

Elizabeth took the stairs two at a time. "I have keys now," she said to Jim, trying each one. Some fit into the lock, but wouldn't turn. Others wouldn't even fit. She felt a little give when she inserted a short key that was almost swallowed by the keyhole, but it didn't release the lock. The next key was hard to turn, but finally the lock sprang open.

When Elizabeth opened the door, Jim tumbled out, hands and feet tied, a piece of duct tape across his mouth. "This may hurt," she said, grabbing a corner of the tape, turning her head, and pulling. It made a ripping sound as it came loose.

"Untie me, then get out of here. Tony is coming back and I don't want you here." Jim sat up and turned his back to Elizabeth, wiggling his fingers.

"The knots are too tight," she said, trying to undo them.

"Then cut the ropes," said Jim.

"With what?" Elizabeth's hands were so sweaty she could hardly hold on to the rope at all.

"A knife. Go get one out of the kitchen."

Again Elizabeth made a flying trip to the kitchen and back. "Did you get in touch with the lawyer?" she asked as she sawed at the rope.

"There's no new will," said Jim. "She'd called and made an appointment, but Gran died before she could actually sign it."

"But the letter. Can't the lawyer use the letter to do what your grandmother wanted?"

"Maybe. She said she wanted to see it, but when I got back here, Tony was waiting. He parked his car someplace else and surprised me. I should have been more careful." Once Jim's hands were free, he grabbed the knife and quickly hacked through the rope binding his feet.

"Tony did this to you?" Elizabeth stepped back. She could see deep lines where the ropes had pressed into the flesh of Jim's wrists. There was a bruise across one cheek, and she was sure that under his socks his ankles would look like his wrists.

"The bruises are from when I rolled down the stairs. I tried to scoot, but it didn't work. It was slow, and I was afraid you'd leave before I could get your attention."

"Still …" Elizabeth reached out with one finger and gently rubbed the lines on his wrist.

"Go! Now," said Jim, pushing her away. "Tony is coming back for me and some more books. He found the letter from Gran about the trust fund, so there's nothing left for me to do but run away."

"You can't do that. I know Mom and Don will help you. Come home with me. Please," Elizabeth pleaded.

"Go. I mean it, or I'll tie you up and leave you for Tony," said Jim. "I'm going to grab some of the books and some of Gran's jewelry. Not everyone is as worried about stuff being stolen as Teresa is. That'll give me some traveling money."

"I have some money at home. Let me give that to you," said Elizabeth. "It's not much, but it'll buy you a few meals."

Jim shook his head. "You've done so much for

me already. I wish I had a sister just like you," he said in a soft voice.

Tears ran down Elizabeth's face. She didn't try to stop them. "I saw the letter too. I'll tell the lawyer …"

The slamming of a car door cut off Elizabeth's words. "It's him," Jim said. "The attic's no good anymore because he has a key. In there, quick!"

They ducked into the pink bedroom, the one Elizabeth thought of as hers, and scooted into a closet that was set under the eaves. It wasn't very deep, and though Elizabeth could stand, Jim had to hunker over.

Tony's footsteps echoed. Each step resounded like a slap, making Elizabeth flinch. When he reached the landing, the sounds ceased, until a series of curses exploded. Elizabeth was so nervous, she almost bolted out of the closet. She wrapped her arms around herself, trying to stop the shaking inside. Even across a dark closet, she knew Jim was looking at her as if she were crazy.

Tony's feet pounded against the wooden stairs, going down this time.

"Stay here," Jim ordered in a firm whisper. "I'm going to distract him so you can get away."

"I'll get help," she said.

Jim opened the closet door carefully, checked the room, then stepped out. "Wait until you hear us talking, then go down the back way."

Elizabeth closed her eyes and prayed. Dear Jesus, please watch over Jim and keep him safe. You're all he has left.

An evil-sounding laugh reached Elizabeth's ears. She tiptoed out of the closet to the rear stairs, pausing to try to hear what Jim and Mr. James were saying. She thought she heard *police, juvenile hall, liar.*

Creeping down the back stairs, Elizabeth tried to think of a way to rescue Jim. No one would make him go back to live with someone who had treated him the way Mr. James had. She was sure that her mother wouldn't. They were going to move into this big house with lots of empty bedrooms. Jim could stay with them. It was such a perfect idea, she didn't know why she hadn't thought of it before. She'd always wanted a big brother.

"Your little girlfriend, where is she?" drifted up the stairs to Elizabeth's ears. She ducked into the apartment, then leaned against the door. How could she get herself and Jim out of this situation? Footsteps, heavier than Jim's in his rubber-soled tennis shoes, passed by the apartment.

Elizabeth's heart pounded so loudly, she thought that it would soon give away her hiding place. She took a deep breath to calm herself and focused on a point of jumbled color across the room, breathing in and out slowly. The calmer she got, the clearer her focus became. She could see each swirl of color on each marble in the clear glass jar—blue, green, red, orange. Marbles!

Opening the apartment door a crack, Elizabeth listened as Mr. James went from room to room, slamming doors against the wall and scooting furniture across the wooden floors. Finally, he started down the narrow stairs. Elizabeth closed the door, waiting.

The rap of his boots ceased. Elizabeth held her breath as she leaned into the door, knowing that she wouldn't be able to stop Mr. James from opening the apartment door if he tried. Then the sound of his footsteps picked up again, receding as he walked down the stairs.

As soon as Elizabeth was sure he had passed, she threw the apartment door open and emptied the jar of marbles onto the stairway. They rolled merrily down the stairs. Mr. James turned and started toward Elizabeth. Immediately he stepped on one of the marbles, teetered for a moment, then his feet flew out from under him. Mr. James' arms shot out, and Elizabeth heard a sickening crack when his total weight landed on his right hand.

It became very quiet for a moment, then Mr. James let out a yowl full of pain. "You brat!" followed the cry. He rolled over onto his back and cradled his arm against his chest. His face was a pale green, already dotted with beads of sweat. Jim stood at the foot of the staircase looking up.

"You'd better call 911," said Elizabeth. "Mr. James fell down the stairs, and I think he broke his arm."

12 A BROTHER AT A BARGAIN PRICE

Elizabeth almost didn't recognize Don's passenger when the black Volvo station wagon pulled into the driveway of the duplex. "Jim, you got your hair cut!" she said.

Jim grinned as he got out of the car, then opened the back door and pulled out cardboard boxes. Mike ran out of the house, plopped a box on his head, and ran back inside without a word.

"We need those," said Elizabeth. "It's amazing how much stuff we've accumulated. It's a good thing we're moving to a bigger house. That means we can keep on accumulating."

"Don't think you're going to use all those boxes!" Aunt Nan picked up as many as she could carry. "I need to pack some things too. Hi, Jim. I baked some peanut butter cookies this afternoon. They're probably still warm if you're hungry. We need to put a little weight on you."

"I never gain weight, no matter how much I eat. I tried to tell you," Jim said, picking up his own load of boxes. "I'll come help you pack your stuff if you want." As soon as Jim had met Aunt Nan, they'd hit it off. He told Elizabeth later that she reminded him of his grandmother.

Elizabeth and Don followed, going into the Bryan's side of the duplex.

"How did it go with the lawyer?" Mom met them in the entryway, taking boxes and tossing them into the living room.

"Mr. James is agreeable to the adoption ..."

Mom clapped her hands, grabbed Elizabeth, and gave her a tight hug.

"... for a small fee," Don finished, folding his arms across his chest and shaking his head. "He wants a couple of the first editions. I said Jim had to agree to the books he chose."

Elizabeth hadn't believed that Mr. James could sink any lower, but with this news she knew he had found a way.

"You said yes, didn't you?" asked Mom.

"Of course I did. There's lots of red tape that we have to go through, but for now, I've been named Jim's legal guardian," said Don.

Thank You, Jesus, Elizabeth prayed. As soon as she'd told Mom and Don about Jim and Mr. James, they'd insisted that Jim stay with Don until things were settled. Mr. James threatened to sue Mom because Elizabeth threw the marbles onto the steps, causing him to fall and break his arm. Then he threatened to have Jim placed in a foster home or juvenile hall, and he threatened to make their lives miserable. But Don had spoken to him and issued a few threats of his own. After that, Mr. James' attitude had changed for the better.

After Jim had stayed with Don for several weeks, starting school at North a grade ahead of Elizabeth, Don and Mom had asked him if he wanted to make the arrangement permanent. Jim had given them an immediate yes.

"Hey, sis!" Jim came into the entryway and picked up a few of the boxes stacked at Elizabeth's feet. "Quit slacking. If there's nothing for you to do over here, come help Aunt Nan."

"Those are my boxes," said Elizabeth, grabbing one.

"You've already filled your share. Anything that doesn't fit in the thousand boxes you've already packed doesn't need to go." Jim pulled.

"Give me that box!" Elizabeth jerked and the cardboard ripped.

"Stop it, both of you," Mom scolded. "There's too much work to do around here to fool around."

When she talked to him like that, a smile lit up Jim's face.

"You're in trouble. She's mad at us," Elizabeth said. "Don't you get it?"

"I like it," said Jim. "Is it okay if I finish helping Aunt Nan?"

"Are there any cookies left?" Don asked. Jim nodded. "I'll help too." Don threw his arm over Jim's shoulders and they headed to Aunt Nan's.

"If Aunt Nan wasn't going to move with us, I'm not sure whether Jim would either," said Elizabeth.

"They've hit it off pretty well. Of course, the two of you sound like you've been brother and sister forever. And Mike has to do everything Jim does." Mom shook her head, but she was smiling too. "I don't know what I'm going to do with three of you."

"Maybe you'll have to have four or five kids. Then you'll be so busy, you won't have time to worry about us anymore," Elizabeth teased.

"The laundry alone would do me in," Mom said. "Go finish packing. Don wants all our stuff ready to go early in the morning so we can load it on the moving van and get it over to the new house by lunchtime. Is Justin still going to help?"

"And Meghan and Rich and Christy and Amy Catherine," said Elizabeth. "Teresa's even coming over to look at those books Jim wants to have appraised. She thinks *Little Women* and *Greasy Creek* are worth a lot of money. The whole day will be like a party."

"Just a little party. Don't forget the big celebration will be next month." Mom hummed a few bars of the "Wedding March."

"You won't let me forget," said Elizabeth. "A new brother and a new stepfather. How blessed can a girl get?"

"She can have me for a mom." Mom put her arm around Elizabeth and they walked up the steps to finish packing for the move.